Daddy's girl

ISBN-13: 978-0-8249-5681-3

Published by WorthyKids/Ideals
An imprint of Worthy Publishing Group
A division of Worthy Media, Inc.
Nashville, Tennessee

Text copyright © 2017 by Helen Foster James
Art copyright © 2017 by Worthy Media, Inc.

Library of Congress CIP data on file

Designed by Georgina Chidlow

Printed and bound in China
RRD-SZ_Jan17_1

Daddy's girl

Written by

Helen Foster James

Illustrated by

Estelle Corke

WorthyKids
ideals®

Nashville, Tennessee

Little Bear, it's time for tea.
Table's set for one...
two...
three!

I think teas
are just **the best.**

daddy's
chair ★

Can you guess
who'll be my guest?

daddy's
chair

Silver tray
and lacy lace.

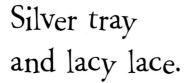

Flowers
in a lovely vase.

Tasty treats
and ooh-la-la.
Fancy teas are
la
tea
dah!

Hats and heels with
**ribbons,
bows.**

**Shiny
Shoes**
for twinkle-toes.

Boa, Crown—
they're just for you.

glitter, bling, and sequins too.

Oh, my, my!
We're quite a sight.
Shimmer, shine,
and Sparkle
bright.

That's his knock.
My daddy'S here!

tea
party
today

Be my guest
and sit right there.

Welcome
to my special tea.

glad you're here
to be with me!

Here's a hat
I made for you—
hearts and dots
with stripes of blue.

HandSome you
and Splendid me.
Now it's time
to have our tea!

Dainty
cups
with tea to pour.

Sugar?
Cream?
Let's have some more.

Tea and
cakes,
we'll each have some—

Sip, Sip, Sip,
and
yum, yum, yum!

Teas are great,
is what I think.

I like these,
with green
and pink.

Which ones do
you love the best?
Purple, white, or all the rest?

You know what,
Daddy, Bear?
We have lots,
so we should Share.

Join us, please, my turtle, frog,

wooly lamb, and fluffy dog.

Sit right here,
my monkey,
cat,

tiny pig,
and flying
bat.

Daddy, friends,
with thankful me.
What a day for
Sharing tea.

Here's a hug,
my daddy dear.
I just love
that you are here.

Love and hugs,
and kisses too.

Daddy,
tea is best with YOU.